JACK & THE BEANSTALK

A Book of Nursery Stories

chosen and edited by

KATHLEEN LINES

and illustrated by

HAROLD JONES

OXFORD
UNIVERSITY
PRESS

OXFORD
UNIVERSITY PRESS

Great Clarendon Street, Oxford OX2 6DP

Oxford University Press is a department of the University of Oxford.
It furthers the University's objective of excellence in research,
scholarship, and education by publishing worldwide in

Oxford   New York

Auckland   Cape Town   Dar es Salaam   Hong Kong   Karachi
Kuala Lumpur   Madrid   Melbourne   Mexico City   Nairobi
New Delhi   Shanghai   Taipei   Toronto

With offices in

Argentina   Austria   Brazil   Chile   Czech Republic   France   Greece
Guatemala   Hungary   Italy   Japan   Poland   Portugal   Singapore
South Korea   Switzerland   Thailand   Turkey   Ukraine   Vietnam

Oxford is a registered trade mark of Oxford University Press
in the UK and in certain other countries

© Oxford University Press 1960

Database right Oxford University Press (maker)

First published 1960
Reprinted 1966, 1970
First Published in this edition 2015

British Library Cataloguing in Publication Data

Data available

ISBN 978-0-19-273587-4 (hardback)
ISBN 978-0-19-273589-8 (slipcase edition)
ISBN 978-0-19-273588-1 (paperback)

10 9 8 7 6 5 4 3 2 1

Printed in China

Acknowledgement

The editor would like to thank Messrs. Frederick Warne and Co. Ltd.
for permission to include *Tom Thumb* from *The Golden Goose Book*

Paper used in the production of this book is a natural, recyclable product made from wood
grown in sustainable forests. The manufacturing process conforms to the environmental
regulations of the country of origin.

Contents

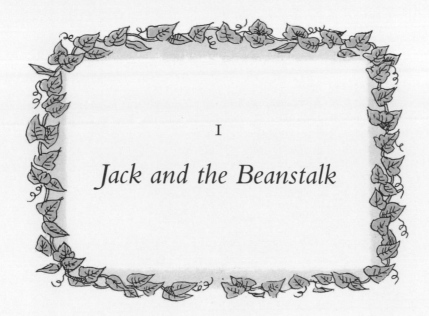

I

Jack and the Beanstalk

Jack and the Beanstalk

Once upon a time there was a poor widow who lived in a cottage in the country, a long distance from London. She had an only child named Jack, and owned one cow whom she called Milky-white. And all that they had to live on was the milk that the cow gave them, and which Jack carried to the market every day to sell.

One morning Milky-white gave no milk. The poor woman was in despair.

'What shall we do?' she cried. 'I have not money enough to buy a bit of bread for another day: nothing remains but my poor cow, and she must now be sold or we shall starve.'

'Cheer up, Mother,' said Jack. 'I'll go and get work somewhere.'

'You've tried that before, Jack,' said his mother, 'and nobody would keep you.'

For although Jack was a good lad, his wits went wool-gathering, and he often forgot what he was supposed to be doing.

So his poor mother sadly sent him to market to sell Milky-white, and he took the cow's halter in his hand and set off.

'Be sure to get a good price!' his mother called after him.

Jack had not gone far along the road when he met a queer-looking little old man, who said to him:

'Well, Jack, where are you going?'

'I am going to market to sell Milky-white,' replied Jack, 'and then we'll have some money to buy food.'

'You look just the sort of boy to make a good bargain,' said the little man. 'Tell me, do you know how many beans make five?'

'Two in each hand and one in my mouth,' answered Jack, as sharp as a needle.

'That's right!' chuckled the old man, 'and here they are,' and he pulled five strange-looking beans out of his pocket. 'As you are so good at sums, I'll do a deal with you. You give me Milky-white, and you can have my beans.'

'What!' cried Jack. 'My lovely cow for your common beans!'

'But they are not common beans,' said the little old man, looking queerer than ever. 'They are magic beans. If you plant them tonight, in the morning they will have grown right up to the sky.'

Jack could hardly believe his ears.

'Did you say right up to the *sky*?' he asked.

'Right up to the very sky,' repeated the old man. 'And as fair play's a jewel, if they don't, you can have your cow back again.'

'All right,' said Jack, and the next moment he found himself alone on the road with no Milky-white and no halter, and the five beans in his hand.

His mother was watching for him when he reached home.

'You've been very quick,' she said. 'So you sold Milky-white? How much have you brought back?'

'You'll never guess, Mother,' said Jack.

'Five pounds . . . ten pounds . . . fifteen . . . twenty?'

'I knew you'd never guess, Mother. I've got five magic beans . . .'

But his mother was so angry and disappointed that she would not listen to any more of Jack's story. Instead she boxed his ears, sent him supperless to bed, and threw the beans out of the window.

Early in the morning, when Jack got up, he found that his room looked very strange. The sun did not seem to be able to shine in properly through the window: something was shading the light. Jack ran down the stairs and out into the garden, and there he found that the five beans which his mother had thrown out the night before had taken root and sprung up like a great tree. They had strong, thick stalks, which were so entwined that they were like a ladder, and though he looked up he could not see the top of this strange beanstalk, for it seemed lost in the clouds.

Jack called his mother, and told her he was going to climb to the top of the beanstalk. Up he went, climbing and climbing and climbing until he reached the sky. There he saw a white road stretching before him as straight as could be, and he set out to walk along it.

He walked on and on, and on and on again, until he came to a great tall house, with a great tall woman standing on the door-step, stirring a huge black pot of porridge.

'Good morning, mum,' said Jack, who was very hungry, having had no supper the night before, and no time for breakfast that morning. 'Could you kindly give me some breakfast?'

'Breakfast!' cried the great tall woman. 'If it's breakfast you're wanting it's breakfast you'll most likely be yourself! My man is an Ogre, and there's nothing he likes better than boy—a fat boy grilled on toast. You'd better be off before he comes home.'

'Oh, please, mum,' said Jack, 'do give me something to eat. I've had nothing to eat since yesterday morning, and I may as well be grilled as die of hunger!'

The Ogre's wife, who was not altogether bad, took Jack in and gave him a good meal of porridge and milk. He had hardly finished when the whole house began to shake, and thump, thump, thump—the Ogre was coming.

'Gracious,' said the Ogre's wife, 'it's my old man! Whatever shall I do with you? Here, come along quick and hide in the oven,' and she pushed Jack inside her huge oven just in time.

The Ogre was enormous. He had three sheep tied on to his belt, and he threw them on the table and said:

'Here, wife, broil me a couple of these for breakfast. But what's this I smell?' and he began to prowl round the kitchen, muttering to himself:

> '*Fee-fi-fo-fum!*
> *I smell the blood of an Englishman.*
> *Be he alive or be he dead,*
> *I'll grind his bones to make my bread.*'

'Nonsense,' said his wife. 'You only smell the bones of that boy you had for dinner yesterday, and which I'm boiling down for soup. Come, begin your breakfast, the sheep won't be long now.'

So the Ogre sat down to breakfast. When he had finished the two sheep, he fetched from a big chest three bags of shining gold pieces, and began to count them. Soon his great head nodded, he fell asleep and the house rocked with his snores.

Then Jack slipped out of the oven, and as he tiptoed past the Ogre he snatched up one of the bags of gold, and ran all the way back to the top of the beanstalk along the straight, white road, and threw down the heavy bag while he climbed down after it, and found it, of course, in his mother's garden.

Then Jack and his mother knew that the beans were really magic, and that the little old man had not deceived Jack after all.

They lived on the bag of gold for some time, until the day came when there was only one more gold piece in the coffer, so Jack made up his mind to go up the beanstalk once more, and see what he could see.

The next morning he rose up early, and climbed and climbed and climbed up through the clouds to the top of the beanstalk as he had done before. There again was the white road stretching before him as straight as could be, and he set out to walk along it.

Sure enough, at the end of it was the great tall house, and the Ogre's wife was standing at the door.

'Good morning, mum,' said Jack, as bold as brass. 'Would you kindly give me something to eat?'

'Go away,' said the Ogre's wife crossly. 'The last time I gave a boy like you some breakfast he made off with a bag of gold. Why, I believe you are the same boy!'

'That's very strange, mum,' replied Jack, 'I wouldn't be surprised if I could tell you something about that, but I'm too hungry to say a word.'

The Ogre's wife was so filled with curiosity that she let him into the kitchen once more, and gave him a big bowl of porridge. Hardly had he finished it when the house began to tremble, and thump, thump, thump, they heard the Ogre coming.

Everything happened as it did before. In came the Ogre, after his wife had quickly shut Jack up in the oven, with three fat calves strung to his belt. He threw them on the table.

'Quick, wife!' he roared. 'Roast these for my breakfast! I hope the oven is hot?' and he went across to open the oven door.

But the Ogre's wife cried out in a hurry:

'Roast! That will take far too long if you are so hungry! I shall boil them—see how brightly the fire glows!'

So the Ogre left the oven door alone, but he began to prowl round the kitchen, growling:

> *'Fee-fi-fo-fum!*
> *I smell the blood of an Englishman.*
> *Be he alive or be he dead,*
> *I'll grind his bones to make my bread.'*

That was what he always growled when he was angry.

'Rubbish,' said his wife. 'You only smell the bones of that boy you had for dinner yesterday, which I am keeping to grill for you tonight.'

So the Ogre sat down to his enormous meal, and when he had finished he called: 'Wife, bring me my magic hen!' So she brought in a small black hen, which she put down on the kitchen table in front of the Ogre.

Then he said to the hen, 'Lay,' and it at once laid a golden egg. And he said, 'Lay,' again, and there was another beautiful, shining,

golden egg. Then the Ogre's head began to nod, and the house rocked with his snores.

Jack made up his mind that he would have that hen, come what might. He crept out of the oven, seized the hen, and was off out of the door like lightning, but he had forgotten that hens cackle after they have laid an egg, and her cackle woke the Ogre, but by then Jack was well down the long, white road. He got safely to the top of the beanstalk, and climbed down it faster than ever before to show his mother the wonderful hen. Then he said, 'Lay,' and it laid a golden egg, and did this as often as Jack commanded it.

Jack and his mother lived very comfortably on the golden eggs laid by the magic hen, until one day Jack thought he would have another adventure at the top of the beanstalk. So one morning he climbed up through the clouds again, and there was the white road stretching before him, and he set out to walk along it.

But this time he knew better than to ask for breakfast, for the Ogre's wife would be sure to recognize him. So he hid in some bushes near the great house, and when the Ogre's wife came out to draw some water from the well, he slipped in through the door and hid himself inside the copper. He had not been there long before the house began to shake, and thump, thump, thump, he heard the Ogre coming.

This time he had three fat oxen tied to his belt, but his wife had hardly begun to cook them before the Ogre started up and began to shout:

> *'Fee-fi-fo-fum!*
> *I smell the blood of an Englishman.*
> *Be he alive or be he dead,*
> *I'll grind his bones to make my bread.*

I smell him, wife, I smell him!' he cried.

'Well, if you do,' said she, 'you may be sure it's that good-for-nothing boy who stole your bag of gold and your magic hen. He'll be in the oven for sure,' and she opened the oven door, but Jack wasn't there, only some joints of meat cooking and sizzling. So she laughed and said, 'Why, of course, it's the boy you caught last night. How forgetful I am!'

The Ogre sat down and began to eat his breakfast, but he wasn't satisfied, and kept getting up to search the cupboards and behind the doors, but luckily he never looked inside the copper.

When he had finished his enormous meal the Ogre called out:

'Wife, bring me my golden harp!'

And she fetched a little harp and stood it on the table before him. Then the Ogre leant back in his chair and said, 'Sing!' And the golden harp sang beautiful songs to him, and it went on singing long after the Ogre had fallen asleep.

Then Jack crept out of the copper, and tiptoed to the table, and caught up the harp and dashed off with it through the door. But the harp cried out, 'Master, master!' and the Ogre woke up and saw Jack disappearing, and rushed after him. Jack tore along as fast as he could, and luckily had a good start, for the Ogre's stride

was twice as long as Jack's, but even so when Jack came to the top of the beanstalk the Ogre was close behind. Jack flung himself into the branches and began to climb down as fast as he could, while the harp continued to call, 'Master, master!' Half-way down

Jack felt a fearful lurch of the beanstalk and nearly fell out of it, and he knew the Ogre was following him down. So he slithered down the rest of the way and, nearing the bottom, called to his mother: 'Mother, Mother, bring an axe, quick, bring an axe!' and his mother ran out with an axe in her hand just as Jack got to the bottom, and there were the Ogre's legs coming through the clouds. But Jack seized the axe and chopped the beanstalk in two just in time. The Ogre came crashing down to the ground and broke his neck.

Then Jack showed his mother the golden harp, which sang most sweetly, and what with that and the golden eggs laid by the magic hen, they both lived happily ever after.

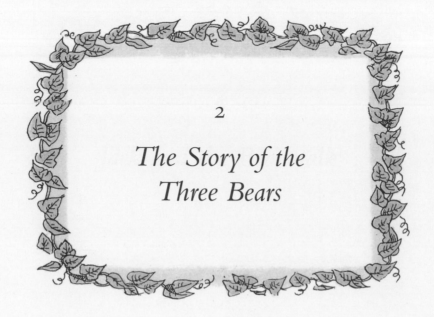

2

*The Story of the
Three Bears*

The Story of the Three Bears

Once upon a time there were Three Bears, who lived together in a house of their own, in a wood. One of them was a Little, Small, Wee Bear, and one was a Middle-sized Bear, and the other was a Great, Huge Bear. They had each a pot for their porridge; a little pot for the Little, Small, Wee Bear, and a middle-sized pot for the Middle Bear, and a great pot for the Great, Huge Bear. And they had each a chair to sit in; a little chair for the Little, Small, Wee Bear, and a middle-sized chair for the Middle Bear, and a great chair for the Great, Huge Bear. And they had each a bed to sleep in; a little bed for the Little, Small, Wee Bear, and a middle-sized bed for the Middle Bear, and a great bed for the Great, Huge Bear.

One day, after they had made the porridge for their breakfast, and poured it into their porridge-pots, they walked out into the wood while the porridge was cooling, that they might not burn their mouths by beginning too soon to eat it. And while they were walking, a little girl called Goldilocks came to the house. First she looked in at the window, and then she peeped in at the keyhole; and seeing nobody in the house, she lifted the latch. The door was not fastened, because the Bears were good Bears, who did nobody any harm, and never suspected that anybody would harm them. So Goldilocks opened the door, and went in; and well pleased she was when she saw the porridge on the table. If she had been a

good little girl, she would have waited till the Bears came home, and then, perhaps, they would have asked her to breakfast; for they were good Bears—a little rough or so, as the manner of Bears is, but for all that very good-natured and hospitable. But she set about helping herself.

So first she tasted the porridge of the Great, Huge Bear, and that was too hot for her. And then she tasted the porridge of the Middle Bear, and that was too cold for her. And then she went to the porridge of the Little, Small, Wee Bear, and tasted that; and that was neither too hot, nor too cold, but just right; and she liked it so well, that she ate it all up.

Then Goldilocks sat down in the chair of the Great, Huge Bear, and that was too hard for her. And then she sat down in the chair of the Middle Bear, and that was too soft for her. And then she sat down in the chair of the Little, Small, Wee Bear, and that was neither too hard, nor too soft, but just right. So she seated herself in it, and there she sat till the bottom of the chair came out, and down she came, plump upon the ground.

Then Goldilocks went upstairs into the bedchamber in which the three Bears slept. And first she lay down upon the bed of the Great, Huge Bear; but that was too high at the head for her. And next she lay down upon the bed of the Middle Bear; and that was too high at the foot for her. And then she lay down upon the bed of the Little, Small, Wee Bear; and that was neither too high at the head, nor too high at the foot, but just right. So she covered herself up comfortably, and lay there till she fell fast asleep.

By this time the Three Bears thought their porridge would be cool enough; so they came home to breakfast. Now Goldilocks had left the spoon of the Great, Huge Bear standing in his porridge.

'SOMEBODY HAS BEEN AT MY PORRIDGE!'
said the Great, Huge Bear, in his great, rough, gruff voice. And when the Middle Bear looked at hers, she saw that the spoon was standing in it too.

'SOMEBODY HAS BEEN AT MY PORRIDGE!'
said the Middle Bear, in her middle voice.

Then the Little, Small, Wee Bear looked at his, and there was the spoon in the porridge-pot, but the porridge was all gone.

'SOMEBODY HAS BEEN AT MY PORRIDGE, AND HAS EATEN
IT ALL UP!'
said the Little, Small, Wee Bear, in his little, small, wee voice.

Upon this the Three Bears, seeing that someone had entered their house, and eaten up the Little, Small, Wee Bear's breakfast, began to look about them.

Now Goldilocks had not put the hard cushion straight when she rose from the chair of the Great, Huge Bear.

'SOMEBODY HAS BEEN SITTING IN MY CHAIR!' said the Great, Huge Bear, in his great, rough, gruff voice.

And Goldilocks had pressed down the soft cushion of the Middle Bear.

'SOMEBODY HAS BEEN SITTING IN MY CHAIR!' said the Middle Bear, in her middle voice.

And you know what Goldilocks had done to the third chair.

'SOMEBODY HAS BEEN SITTING IN MY CHAIR AND HAS SAT THE BOTTOM OF IT OUT!' said the Little, Small, Wee Bear in his little, small, wee voice.

Then the Three Bears thought it necessary that they should make further search; so they went upstairs into their bedchamber. Now Goldilocks had pulled the pillow of the Great, Huge Bear out of its place.

'SOMEBODY HAS BEEN LYING IN MY BED!' said the Great, Huge Bear, in his great, rough, gruff voice.

And Goldilocks had pulled the bolster of the Middle Bear out of its place.

'SOMEBODY HAS BEEN LYING IN MY BED!' said the Middle Bear, in her middle voice.

And when the Little, Small, Wee Bear came to look at his bed, there was the bolster in its place; and the pillow in its place upon the bolster; and upon the pillow was Goldilocks' head—which was not in its place, for she had no business there.

'SOMEBODY HAS BEEN LYING IN MY BED—AND HERE SHE IS!' said the Little, Small, Wee Bear, in his little, small, wee voice.

Little Goldilocks had heard in her sleep the great rough, gruff voice of the Great, Huge Bear, but she was so fast asleep that it was no more to her than the roaring of wind or the rumbling of thunder. And she had heard the middle voice of the Middle Bear, but it was only as if she had heard someone speaking in a dream. But when she heard the little, small, wee voice of the Little, Small, Wee Bear, it was so sharp, and so shrill, that it awakened her at once. Up she started; and when she saw the Three Bears on one side of the bed, she tumbled herself out at the other and ran to the window. Now the window was open, because the Bears, like good, tidy Bears, as they were, always opened their bedchamber window when they got up in the morning. Out jumped Goldilocks and ran off into the wood. What happened to her no one knows, but the Three Bears never set eyes on her again.

3

Cinderella

Cinderella

There was once a man whose wife died and left him to bring up their only child, a little daughter, who was sweet and gentle by nature and as pretty as a girl could be.

Father and daughter lived happily enough together until the man married again. His new wife was a proud and masterful woman, with two plain daughters who were as arrogant and disagreeable as she was herself. These three soon took command in the house and, because they were jealous of the young girl's charm and beauty, they always spoke unkindly to her and made her work from morning till night. She had no pretty dresses, only the cast-off clothes of the older girls; she had to sweep and dust and scrub; to lay the fire; to cook, and wash the dishes. When her work was done the poor child had nowhere to go but the kitchen, where she sat in the chimney-corner among the cinders and ashes; and for this reason she was called Cinderella.

Now it happened that the prince of that country was unmarried. The king, his father, decided to give a great ball to which all persons of consequence were to be invited. The ball would be held for three nights and the king felt sure that his son would be able to find a bride among the beautiful ladies who would attend.

An invitation was received by Cinderella's sisters, who were highly delighted. They spent hours discussing what they should wear, and even consulted Cinderella, for she had excellent taste. Cinderella had to wash and iron and sew for them, and when the great day came she was summoned to help them dress. She did up hooks and eyes, tied ribbons and laces, arranged their hair, and handed them the glittering jewels and ornaments with which they decked themselves—for they were determined to impress the prince with all their finery.

After everyone had gone to the palace and she was left alone poor Cinderella sat down in the chimney-corner and wept bitterly. She would so dearly have liked to have gone to the ball. Suddenly there appeared beside her a little old woman, who smiled at her and asked, 'Cinderella, why are you crying?'

'Oh,' said Cinderella, 'my sisters have gone to a magnificent ball at the palace, and I wish, oh! how I wish they had taken me too!'

'Dry your eyes,' said the little old lady. 'I am your fairy god-mother, and if you promise to do exactly as I tell you, you *shall* go to the ball.'

So Cinderella dried her eyes, and when her godmother told her to fetch a pumpkin, she did so without question. With one touch of her wand the fairy turned the pumpkin into a splendid golden coach. Then she said to Cinderella, 'Go and fetch the mouse-trap.' Inside the trap were six mice and a rat. The fairy godmother quickly turned the mice into six beautiful horses and the rat into a coachman. Six lizards, which Cinderella found for her in the garden, became six footmen in handsome livery.

'There you are,' said the godmother, 'now you can go to the ball!'

'But what shall I wear?' asked Cinderella. 'I can't go in these old rags, and I have no other dress.'

'That is soon put right,' answered her godmother. She touched

Cinderella with her wand, and at once her old clothes fell away
and Cinderella was beautiful to behold in a gown of shimmering
silk all studded with precious stones. Her godmother then gave
her a pair of glass slippers, the prettiest little slippers ever seen. Then
Cinderella stepped into the golden coach but, before she drove off
to the ball, her godmother gave her a solemn warning.

'You must be sure to leave before midnight. If you stay one
minute after twelve o'clock, everything will become as it was
before. Your coach will turn back into a pumpkin, your horses and
retainers into mice and lizards, and you will be dressed in your old
rags again.'

Cinderella promised. She thanked her fairy godmother and
drove off full of joy to the palace.

When she arrived she was met by the prince himself, and entered the ballroom on his arm. Everyone stopped dancing, even the musicians ceased to play, so struck were they by the grace and beauty of this new-comer, whom they took to be some foreign princess. The prince danced several times with her and hardly took his eyes off her the whole evening. During supper Cinderella was at pains to be gracious to her two sisters, for, although splendidly dressed, they were still plain and awkward and few people had asked to dance with them.

Soon after half-past eleven, remembering her promise to her godmother, Cinderella made a graceful curtsy to the king and the queen and the prince, and quietly took her leave. She was safely back home, and in her accustomed place by the kitchen fire, some time before her sisters returned.

'How late you are,' she said as she opened the door to them, yawning and rubbing her eyes, as though she had just awakened from sleep.

'If you had been at the ball you would not have been home any earlier,' one of them answered. 'A beautiful princess was there and no one left before she did.'

'She was vastly agreeable to us,' added the other. 'The prince himself was much taken with her; he had eyes for no one else.'

The two sisters were full of admiration for the strange princess who had so outshone every other beauty at the ball.

The next evening the two sisters went again to the palace. Cinderella went also, and looked even more lovely than she had done the night before. The king's son was constantly at her side, and she enjoyed herself so much that she almost forgot her godmother's warning. It was so nearly midnight by the time she left the ball that she had barely time to reach home before her finery disappeared.

When they returned, her sisters had much to say about the strange princess whose name nobody knew. The prince, they said, was very much in love with her, and had said he would give all he possessed to find out who she was.

The third night Cinderella's dress was cloth of gold and silver; it was trimmed with diamonds, and she wore a diamond circlet in her hair. Everyone at the palace waited for the arrival of the

unknown beauty; the ball did not start until she came. This time the prince danced with no one else, and he stayed beside Cinderella the whole evening. In her happiness Cinderella had not a care in

the world. The hours sped by and she was dancing with the prince when the clock began to strike. Surely it was only eleven? But the strokes boomed out—ten, eleven, twelve! Midnight! In horror

Cinderella wrenched her hand from the prince's grasp. She darted through the doorway and as she ran down the great staircase, she lost one of her little glass slippers, but she was in too much of a hurry to stop and pick it up. By the time she reached the bottom of the stairs her beautiful dress had turned to rags and when she reached the door, coach, horses, coachman and footmen had all vanished. Cinderella had to run all the way home. She arrived panting and out of breath with nothing left of her magnificence except one little glass slipper.

What a to-do there was at the palace! When she sprang so suddenly from his grasp the prince had tried to follow, but he soon lost sight of Cinderella in the crowd, and could not tell which way she had gone. None of the guards whom he questioned had seen the beautiful princess; one of them had caught sight of a little ragged girl running through the palace grounds, but of the princess there was not a sign. The prince was in despair. Then one of the courtiers brought to him the little glass slipper which had been found on the great stairway. He persuaded the king to make a proclamation and send heralds through the land to announce that the prince would marry the lady to whom the slipper belonged, and that everyone, high and low, would have a chance to try it on until the right owner was found.

The slipper was carried first to the princesses, then to the duchesses, and then to every member of the Court. But all in vain. Finally it was brought to the house of the two sisters, who did all they could to fit it on, but could not manage it. Cinderella, who was watching them, and who recognized her slipper, said,

'Let us see if it will fit me!'

The sisters began to laugh and to jeer at her. But the Gentleman of the Court who was trying on the slipper had seen how lovely she was, and he said that certainly she should try, for he had orders to try it on all the girls in the land. He made Cinderella sit down, and slid the slipper on to her little foot, and saw that it fitted her as if it had been made for her. The two sisters were amazed, but were even more astonished when Cinderella pulled out of her pocket the other little slipper and put it on. At that moment her fairy godmother appeared. She touched Cinderella's clothes with her wand, and they became even more magnificent than any she had worn before.

The two sisters now recognized her as the beautiful princess they had seen at the ball. They threw themselves at her feet to crave her pardon for their unkindness to her. Cinderella raised them up, and, kissing them, told them that she forgave them with all her heart, and only desired them to love her always.

She was conducted to the young prince, arrayed as she was. He thought she was more lovely than ever, and married her a few days afterwards. Cinderella, who was as good as she was beautiful, brought her two sisters to live at the palace, and married them on the very same day to two great lords of the Court.

4

The Golden Goose

50

The Golden Goose

There was once a man who had three sons. Two were bright, clever lads but the youngest, because he was slow and quieter than his brothers, was thought to be stupid. He was called Dummling, which means Simpleton, and was despised and laughed at by the whole family.

Now it happened one day that the eldest son was to go into the forest to cut wood. His mother baked him a delicious cake and gave him a bottle of wine to take with him, so that he might not suffer from hunger and thirst. When he came to the wood he met a little old man, who, bidding him good day, said: 'Give me a small piece of cake, and let me drink a mouthful of your wine; I am so hungry and thirsty.' But the clever son answered: 'If I were to give you my cake and wine, I should have none for myself, so be off with you,' and he left the little man standing there, and walked away. He was soon to pay for his rudeness for hardly had he begun to chop down a tree, when his axe slipped and cut his arm, so that he had to go home at once and have the wound bound up.

Thereupon the second son went into the wood, and his mother gave him, as she had given to the eldest, a sweet cake and a bottle of wine. The little old man met him also, and begged for a small slice of cake and a drink of wine. But the second son spoke out quite plainly: 'What I give to you I lose myself—be off with you,' and he left the little man standing there, and walked on.

Punishment was not long in coming to him, for he had made but two strokes at a tree when he cut his leg and had to make the best of his way home.

Then Dummling said: 'Father, let me go into the forest and chop wood.' But his father answered him: 'Your brothers have done themselves much harm, so as you understand nothing about wood-cutting you had better not try.' But Dummling begged for so long that at last his father said: 'Well, go if you like; experience will soon make you wiser.' To him his mother gave a cake, but it was made with flour and water and had been baked in the ashes, and with it she gave him a bottle of sour beer. When he came to the wood the little man met him also, and greeted him, and said: 'Give me a slice of your cake and a drink from your bottle; I am so hungry and thirsty.' Dummling replied: 'I have only a cake that has been baked in the ashes, and some sour beer, but if that will satisfy you, let us sit down and eat together.' So they sat themselves down, and as Dummling pulled out his cinder-cake it was a fine

rich cake, and the sour beer became good wine. So they ate and drank together, and when the meal was finished, the little man said: 'As you have a good heart and are willing to share what you have, I will grant you good luck. Yonder stands an old tree; cut it down, and in its roots you will find

something.' Saying this the old
man took his departure, and
Dummling set about chopping
down the tree. When it
fell, there among its roots sat
a goose, with feathers of pure gold.

He lifted her up, and carrying her with him, went on to an inn
where he intended to stay the night.

Now the innkeeper had three daughters; and when they saw the
goose they were curious to know what wonderful kind of a bird
it could be, and longed to have one of its golden feathers. The
eldest daughter said to herself, 'I must and will have a feather'; and
so when Dummling had gone out, she seized the goose by the
wing. But there her hand stuck fast! Shortly afterwards the second
daughter came, intending to pluck a feather, too. But the moment
she touched her sister, she also stuck fast. And lastly came the third
daughter, who also wanted a golden feather. When the others saw
her they cried out, 'Keep off, for goodness' sake, keep off!' But
she, not understanding why they told her to keep away, thought
to herself, 'If they go to the goose, why should not I?' She ran
forward, but as she touched her sister she too stuck fast, and pull as

she might she could not get away. And thus they had all to pass the night beside the goose.

The next morning Dummling took the goose under his arm and went on his way, without troubling himself at all about the three girls who were hanging to the bird. There they went, always running behind him, now to the right, now to the left, whichever way he chose to go. In the middle of the fields they met a parson, and when he saw the procession he called out, 'Shame on you, you bold girls, to run after a young fellow in this way! Come, leave go!' With this he caught the youngest by the hand, and tried to pull her back, but when he touched her he found he could not get away, and he too must needs run behind. Then the sexton came along, and saw the parson following on the heels of the three girls.

This so astonished him that he called out, 'Hi! your Reverence, whither away so fast? Do you forget that today we have a christening?' Then he ran after the parson and caught him by the coat, but he too remained sticking fast.

As the five now ran on, one behind the other, two labourers who were returning from the field with their tools, came along. The parson called out to them and begged that they would set him and the sexton free. No sooner had they touched the sexton, than they too had to hang on, and now there were seven running after Dummling and his goose.

In this way they came to a city where a king reigned who had an only daughter, who was so serious that no one could make her laugh. Therefore he had announced that whoever should make

her laugh should have her for his wife. When Dummling heard this he went with his goose and all its train before the king's daughter, and when she saw the seven people all running behind each other, she began to laugh, and she laughed and laughed till it seemed as though she could never stop. Thereupon Dummling asked to have her for his wife. The king was not best pleased to have a simple lad like Dummling for his son-in-law, but at last consented and the wedding was celebrated with great splendour. When the king died Dummling inherited the kingdom, and he lived long and happily with his bride.

5

Little Red Riding-Hood

Little Red Riding-Hood

Once upon a time there was a little girl who was called little Red Riding-Hood, because she so often wore a red cape and hood which her grandmother had made for her.

One day her mother said, 'Come, my dear, put on your cape and hood and go and see how your grandmother is, for I hear she has been taken ill. Take her this cake that I have just baked and this pot of fresh butter.'

Little Red Riding-Hood liked visiting her grandmother so, with the cake and butter in a little basket, she set off at once. Her way lay through a wood, and as she set off her mother called: 'Now, be sure to keep to the path, and don't loiter by the wayside.'

But there was so much to see in the wood that little Red Riding-Hood soon forgot to hurry. She left the path and ran about under the trees, trying to catch the bright butterflies that fluttered among

the flowers and tall grasses. At last she came to a clearing where some wood-cutters were at work, and there she met a wolf.

Now the hungry wolf would have eaten little Red Riding-Hood but he was afraid of the wood-cutters. So he only stopped and spoke to her politely. 'Good day, little Red Riding-Hood. Where are you going?'

'I'm going to see my grand-mother who is ill,' answered little Red Riding-Hood, 'and I am taking her this butter and cake.'

'Does she live a long way off?'

asked the wolf. 'She lives at the other side of the wood,' said little Red Riding-Hood, 'in the first cottage beyond the mill.'

Then the wicked wolf decided he would also visit the grandmother, but he would get there before little Red Riding-Hood did. So he pretended to go on his way, but as soon as he was out of sight, he quickly turned on to

the straight path and soon reached the grandmother's cottage.
Rap, rap, rap! He knocked on the door.

'Who's there?' called the grandmother, who was in bed.

'Little Red Riding-Hood,' answered the wolf, trying as best he could to disguise his gruff voice. 'I've come to bring you a cake and some butter, and to ask how you are.'

'Pull the bobbin, and the latch will go up,' said the grandmother.

So the wolf pulled the bobbin and the latch went up. In went the wolf, and in next to no time he'd gobbled up the old lady.

Then he shut the door, put on the old grandmother's night-cap, and got into bed to wait for little Red Riding-Hood.

Presently along came little Red Riding-Hood, who had lingered by the way to pick a big bunch of flowers.

She knocked on the door, rap, rap, rap!

'Who's there?' said the wolf.

Little Red Riding-Hood was surprised to hear the wolf's gruff voice, but she thought her grandmother must have a cold; so she answered:

'Little Red Riding-Hood, and I've brought you a cake and some butter.'

'Pull the bobbin, and the latch will go up,' said the wolf.

Little Red Riding-Hood pulled the bobbin, and up went the latch, and little Red Riding-Hood went into the cottage.

The cunning old wolf was tucked up in bed, with the bed-clothes pulled high round his chin. He tried to make his voice soft.

'Come and kiss me, my dear,' said he.

Little Red Riding-Hood went up to the bed.

'Oh, grandmamma,' she said, 'what big arms you've got.'
'All the better to hug you with, my dear,' said the wolf.
'And grandmamma, what big ears you've got!'
'All the better to hear you with, my dear.'
'Oh, grandmamma, what big eyes you've got!'
'All the better to see you with, my dear.'
'But, grandmamma, what big teeth you've got!'
'All the better to eat you with!' cried the wolf, and with that he sprang out of bed to gobble up little Red Riding-Hood.

But just at that moment, in came one of the wood–cutters. He killed the wicked wolf with one blow from his axe, and then he took little Red Riding-Hood safely home to her mother.

6

The Sleeping Beauty

The Sleeping Beauty

Once upon a time there lived a king and queen who had no children; and this they lamented very much. But one day as the queen was walking by the side of the river, a little fish lifted its head out of the water, and said, 'Your wish shall be fulfilled, and you shall soon have a daughter.'

What the little fish had foretold soon came to pass; and the queen had a little girl who was so very beautiful that the king could not cease looking on her for joy, and determined to hold a great feast. So he invited not only his relations, friends and neighbours, but also all the fairies, that they might be kind and good to his little daughter. Now there were thirteen fairies in his kingdom and he had only twelve golden dishes for them to eat out of, so he was obliged to leave one of the fairies without an invitation. The rest came, and after the feast was over they gave all their best gifts to the little princess: one gave her virtue, another beauty, another riches, and so on till she had all that was excellent in the world. When eleven had done blessing her, the thirteenth, who had not been invited, and was very angry on that account, came in, and determined to take her revenge. So she cried out, 'The king's daughter shall in her fifteenth year be wounded by a spindle, and fall down dead.'

Then the twelfth, who had not yet given her gift, came forward and said that the bad wish must be fulfilled, but that she could soften it, and that the king's daughter should not die, but fall asleep for a hundred years.

But the king hoped to save his dear child from the threatened evil, and ordered that all the spindles in the kingdom should be bought up and destroyed. All the fairies' gifts were in the meantime fufilled; for the princess was so beautiful, and well-behaved, and amiable, and wise, that everyone who knew her loved her. Now it happened that on the very day she was fifteen years old the king and queen were not at home, and she was left alone in the palace. So she roved about by herself, and looked at all the rooms and chambers, till at last she came to an old tower, to which there was a narrow staircase ending with a little door. In the door there was a golden key, and when she turned it the door sprang open, and there sat an old lady spinning away very busily.

'Why, how now, good mother,' said the princess, 'what are you doing there?'

'Spinning,' said the old lady, and nodded her head.

'How prettily that little thing turns round!' said the princess, and took the spindle and began to spin. But scarcely had she touched it before the prophecy was fulfilled, and she fell down lifeless on the ground.

However, she was not dead, but had only fallen into a deep sleep; and the king and queen, who just then came home, and all their court, fell asleep, too; and the horses slept in the stables, and the dogs in the court, the pigeons on the house-top and the flies on the walls. Even the fire on the hearth left off blazing, and went to sleep; and the meat that was roasting stood still; and the cook who was at that moment pulling the kitchen-boy by the hair to give

him a box on the ear for something he had done amiss, let him go, and both fell asleep; and so everything stood still, and slept soundly.

A large hedge of thorns soon grew round the palace, and every year it became higher and thicker, till at last the whole palace was surrounded and hidden, so that not even the roof or the chimneys could be seen. But there went a report through all the land of the beautiful sleeping Rose-Bud (for so was the king's daughter called);

so that from time to time several kings' sons came, and tried to break through the thicket into the palace. This they could never do; for the thorns and bushes laid hold of them as it were with hands, and there they stuck fast and died miserably.

After many, many years there came a king's son into that land, and an old man told him the story of the thicket of thorns, and how a beautiful palace stood behind it in which was a wondrous princess, called Rose-Bud, asleep with all her court. He told, too, how he had heard from his grandfather that many, many princes had come, and tried to break through the thicket, but had stuck fast and died.

Then the young prince said, 'All this shall not frighten me. I will go and see Rose-Bud.'

The old man tried to dissuade him, but he persisted in going.
Now that very day were the hundred years completed; and as
the prince came to the thicket, he saw nothing but beautiful
flowering shrubs, through which he passed with ease, and they
closed after him as firm as ever. Then he came at last to the palace,

and there in the court lay the dogs asleep, and the horses in the stables, and on the roof sat the pigeons fast asleep with their heads under their wings; and when he came into the palace, the flies slept on the walls, and the cook in the kitchen was still holding up her hand as if she would beat the boy, and a maid sat with a black fowl in her hand ready to be plucked.

Then he went on still farther, and all was so still that he could

hear every breath he drew; till at last he came to the old tower and opened the door of the little room in which Rose-Bud was; and there she lay fast asleep, and looked so beautiful that he could not take his eyes off her, and he stooped down and gave her a kiss. But the moment he kissed her she opened her eyes and awoke, and smiled upon him. Then they went out together, and presently the king and queen also awoke, and all the court, and they gazed on each other with great wonder. And the horses got up and shook themselves, and the dogs jumped about and barked; the pigeons took their heads from under their wings, and looked about and flew into the fields; the flies on the walls buzzed away; the fire in the kitchen blazed up and cooked the dinner, and the roast meat turned round again; the cook gave the boy a box on the ear so that he cried out, and the maid went on plucking the fowl. And then was the wedding of the prince and Rose-Bud celebrated, and they lived happily together all their lives long.

7

Tom Tit Tot

Tom Tit Tot

Once upon a time there was a woman and she baked five pies. But when they came out of the oven they were over-baked, and the crust was far too hard. So the woman said to her daughter:

'Daughter,' says she, 'put the pies on the shelf and leave' em there, and with time they'll come again.'

By that, you know, she meant that the crust would become softer. But her daughter, she says to herself, 'If the pies will come again, why shouldn't I eat them now?' So, having good teeth, she set to work and ate them all.

Now when supper-time came the woman told her daughter to fetch one of the pies, 'For,' said she, 'they are sure to have come again by now.'

The girl went to see but of course there was nothing on the shelf but the empty pie plates.

So back she came and said, 'No, they've not come again.'

'What, not one of them?' asked the mother, very surprised.

'Not one,' answered the daughter.

'Well, come again, or not come again,' said her mother, 'I must have one of those pies for my supper.'

'But how can you,' says the daughter, 'if they haven't come? And they haven't, as sure's sure.'

'But I can,' says the mother. 'Go at once, my girl, and bring me the best on them.'

'Best or worst,' answered the daughter, 'I've ate the lot, and you *can't* have one till it comes again.'

Well, the woman was fair amazed. She went to see for herself, and, sure enough, there were the empty plates. Her daughter had eaten every one of those pies!

So the woman took her spinning out to the doorstep, sat her down and began to spin. And as she span she sang:

> *'My daughter ha' ate five, five pies today,*
> *My daughter ha' ate five, five pies today,*
> *My daughter ha' ate five pies today.'*

It happened that the king came riding down the street. He heard the woman singing but could not make out the words of the song. So he stopped and asked:

'What are you singing, my good woman?'

Now the woman was ashamed, she did not want the king to know what her daughter had done, so she sang instead:

> *'My daughter ha' spun five, five skeins today,*
> *My daughter ha' spun five, five skeins today,*
> *My daughter ha' spun five skeins today.'*

'Five skeins in a day?' cries the king. 'I've never heard tell of anyone who could do that.' Then after a minute's thought he said, 'See here, good woman, I'm in search of a wife and I'll wed your daughter. For eleven months of the year she'll have all the food she likes to eat, all the gowns she likes to wear and all the company she cares to keep, *but* in the twelfth month she must spin five skeins every day; if she does not she must die. Come, is it a bargain?'

The woman agreed. She thought what a grand marriage it would be for her daughter. And as for the five skeins—well, there would be time enough to find some way out of that part of the bargain. Likely as not, the king would have forgotten all about it long before eleven months had passed.

So they were married. And the girl was happy as happy could be. She had all the food she liked to eat, all the gowns she liked to wear, and all the company she cared to keep, and the king was kind to her. But as time passed and the eleventh month drew near, she began to think of those five skeins. But not a word did the king say about them; so she hoped he had quite forgotten.

But on the very last day of the eleventh month he took her into a room she had never set eyes on before. It had one window and there was nothing in it but a spinning-wheel, a stool and a narrow bed.

'Now, my dear,' says he, 'you will be shut in here tomorrow morning with some victuals and some flax, and if by night-fall you have not spun five skeins, your head will come off.'

She was very frightened, for she had always been a gatless, thoughtless girl and she did not know how to spin at all. What was she to do on the next day with no one to help her? She sat down on a stool and cried and cried and cried.

Then, as she sat sobbing and crying, she heard a queer little knocking at the bottom of the door.

So she upped and opened the door, and what should she see but a small little black thing. It had a long tail which it twirled round.

That said, 'What are you crying for?'

'What's that to you?' says she.

'Never mind,' That said. 'You tell me why you're crying.'

'It won't do me any good if I do,' says she.

'It may,' answered That, twirling its tail round and round.

'Well,' says she, 'it won't do any harm if it doesn't do any good.' So she upped and told all about the pies and the skeins, and all that had happened.

And then that little black thing says, 'If that's all, I can help. I'll come to your window every morning and take the flax, and I'll bring it back spun into five skeins at night.'

'Oh,' says the girl, 'but what is your pay?'

Then That looked out of the corners of That's eyes and said: 'I'll give you three guesses every night to guess my name, and if you haven't guessed it before the month is up, why'—and That twirled That's tail faster than ever—'you shall be mine.'

Well, with three guesses every night for a whole month she felt sure she would be able to come upon the right name, and as there was no other help in sight, she agreed.

The next day the king once more led her to the strange room and set before her a great bundle of flax, and the day's food.

'Now there's the flax, my dear,' says he. 'And don't forget—if it is not all spun by tonight, off goes your head.'

Then he left her and locked the door. Soon she heard a queer knocking at the window. She upped and opened it, and sure enough there was that black thing sitting on the window-ledge.

'Where's the flax?' says he.

'Here it is,' says she.

So she gave That the flax and away he flew. When evening came she heard again that queer knocking at the window. She upped and opened it, and there was that little black thing with five skeins all finely spun.

Then That said, 'Now, what is my name?'

'Is That Bill?' says she.

'Noo, That ain't,' says he.

'Then is That Ned?' says she.

'Noo, That ain't,' says That, and twirled his tail.

'Well,' says she, 'is That Mark?'

'Noo, it ain't,' says he, and laughed and twirled his tail and flew away.

When the king came in, he found the five skeins all ready for him.

'I see I shall not have to order your head off tonight, my dear,' says he. 'You'll have more flax and your food again in the morning.' And then he bade her good night.

Next day another great bundle of flax was brought to her, and the day's food.

Then it happened as before. There was a knocking at the window. When the girl opened it there was the small little black thing. He took the bundle of flax and before night-fall brought back five spun skeins.

And so it went on. Every day she had fresh flax and food, and every day that little black thing used to come mornings and evenings. And all the day long the girl sat thinking up names to say to That when he brought the skeins at night. But she never hit upon the right one. And as it grew towards the end of the month that little black thing looked at her out of the corners of his eyes, and grinned, and That twirled That's tail, faster and faster every time she made a wrong guess.

So it came to the last day but one. The little black thing arrived in the evening with the five skeins of flax all ready spun, and said:

'Have you got That's name yet?'

'Is That Nicodemus?' says she.

'Noo, 't'aint,' That says, and twirled That's tail.

'Is That Samuel?' says she.

'Noo, 't'aint,' That says.

'Well—is That Methuselah?' says she.

'Noo, it t'aint that neither,' says he. Then That fixes her with eyes like coal a-fire, and says, 'There is only tomorrow night, and then you'll be mine.'

And away That flew.

Well, she felt so bad she couldn't even cry; but she heard the king coming, so she hid her worry.

'Well, my dear,' says he, 'I don't doubt you'll have your five skeins again tomorrow night. I reckon you'll keep your head, so let us enjoy ourselves.' Then he ordered the servants to bring food, and another stool for him, and down they sat to supper.

But the poor girl could eat nothing; she could not forget the trouble on her mind. The king hadn't eaten but a mouthful or two when he stops and begins to laugh.

'What's the joke?' says she.

'Why,' says the king, 'When I was out a-hunting today I came to a place in the wood I'd never been in before. There was an old chalk-pit, and out of the chalk-pit I heard a kind of a sort of a humming. So I got off my hobby and went right quiet to the pit and looked down. What should be there but the funniest little black thing you ever set eyes upon. And what was it doing but it had a little spinning-wheel and was spinning away as fast as fast, and twirling its tail. And while it was spinning it kept singing away:

"*Nimmy nimmy not*
My name is Tom Tit Tot."'

Well, when she heard these words the girl nearly jumped out of her skin for joy; but she didn't say a word.

And she said nothing next morning when the little black thing came for the flax, all grinning and maliceful. When night came and she heard That knocking against the window, she upped and opened it. And That came right inside, grinning from ear to ear. And oh, That's tail was twirling round so fast!

'Well,' says That, as he gave her the five skeins, 'what's my name?'

Then she says, pretending to be tearful, 'Is That Solomon?'

'Noo, t'aint,' says That, twirling That's tail and coming farther into the room.

'Well, is That Zebedee?' she says.

'Noo, t'aint,' cried the impet, full of glee. And it stepped forward and stretched out its little black hands to her. And oh, how That twirled That's tail!

'Take your time,' says That, grinning with glee. 'Take time! Next guess and you're mine!'

Well, she backed away from him, and she laughed out loud and pointed her finger at him and said, says she:

> 'Nimmy nimmy not
> Your name is TOM TIT TOT.'

And when That heard her, he gave a shriek and stamped his foot,
and in a flash he had vanished through the window. The girl never
saw him again, and she and the king lived happily ever after.

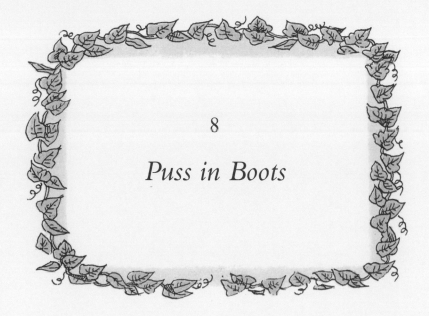

8

Puss in Boots

Puss in Boots

A poor miller left to his three sons all the property he had, which was his mill, his ass, and his cat. The division was soon made: the eldest son had the mill, the second the ass, and the youngest only the cat. This lad was much upset at having so poor a heritage. 'My brothers,' he said, 'could earn a respectable living by joining together; but as for me, when I have eaten my cat, and made a muff out of his skin, there will be nothing left me but to die of hunger.'

The cat, who heard these words, but pretended that he had not done so, put on a wise and thoughtful look, and said: 'Master, do not distress yourself; you have only to give me a sack, and get made for me a pair of boots in which I can go through the brushwood, and you will see that you are not so badly off as you think.'

Although the cat's master did not trust much to this, he had seen him perform many nimble tricks in catching rats and mice (as for instance when he hung by his feet, or hid himself in the flour, pretending to be dead) and he was not without hope of finding the cat of some use in his trouble.

When the cat had what he had asked for, he pulled on the boots, in which he looked very fine; and slinging the sack on his back, he held the strings with his forepaws, and went off to a warren where there lived a great number of rabbits. He put some bran and parsley into his sack, and stretching himself out as if he had been dead, he waited for some young rabbit, not very familiar with the tricks of the world, to come into the sack to eat what was placed there.

He had scarcely lain down before he had his wish. A young madcap of a rabbit crept into the sack, and Master Puss, at once drawing the strings, caught him and killed him. Then, proud of his catch, he went off to the king's palace and asked to have speech with him. He was taken up to his majesty's room, and bowing low to the king on entering, he said: 'Sir, you see here a fine rabbit which the Marquis of Carabas' (that was the name he had chosen to give his master) 'has charged me to present to you on his behalf.'

'Tell your master,' replied the king, 'that I am much obliged to him, and delighted with his present.'

Another day Puss hid himself in a field of corn, keeping his sack open; and when two partridges had hopped into it, he drew the strings and captured them both. He hastened at once to offer them to the king, just as he had done with the rabbit. The king was pleased to accept the birds and ordered a fee to be given to the

cat. So Master Puss went on for two or three months, carrying to the king, from time to time, game which he said was the result of his master's hunting.

One day, when he knew that the king was going for a drive along the river-bank with his daughter, the fairest princess in the world, he said to his master: 'If you would follow my advice, your fortune is made. You have only to bathe in the river at the spot I point out to you, and leave the rest to me!'

The young man did what his cat advised, without knowing what was to come of it. While he was bathing, the king came by; whereupon Puss began to shriek with all his might: 'Help! help! The Marquis of Carabas is drowning!'

At this cry the king looked out of the window of his coach, and recognizing the cat who had brought him so much game, he ordered his guards to run quickly to the help of the Marquis of Carabas. While they were hauling the poor marquis out of the water, the cat drew near to the coach, and told the king that while his master was bathing, some robbers had come and carried off his clothes, though he shouted 'Thieves!' with all his might. The rascal had really hidden them under a big stone.

The king at once ordered the officers of his wardrobe to go and fetch one of his finest suits for the Marquis of Carabas. The king showed him every attention, and as the fine clothes they had just brought gave him a distinguished appearance (for he was a handsome fellow and very well formed), the king's daughter took a great fancy to him, and the marquis had given her no more than

two or three very respectful but rather affectionate glances before she fell in love with him. The king insisted on his getting into the coach, and joining in their drive.

The cat, delighted to see that his plan was proving successful, ran on ahead, and meeting some countrymen mowing a meadow, he said to them: 'My good haymakers, if you don't tell the king that this meadow belongs to the Marquis of Carabas, you shall all be chopped into mince-meat.'

The king did not fail to ask them whose meadow they were mowing.

'It belongs to the Marquis of Carabas,' they said all together, for the cat's threat had scared them.

'That's a fine estate of yours,' said the king to the marquis.

'You see, sir,' said the marquis, 'it's a meadow that never fails to yield excellent grass every year.'

Master Puss, still going on ahead, met some reapers, and said to them: 'My good reapers, if you don't say that all this corn belongs to the Marquis of Carabas, you shall all be chopped into mince-meat.'

The king, who passed by a minute afterwards, wanted to know who was the owner of all the corn that he saw.

'It belongs to the Marquis of Carabas,' said the reapers, and the king congratulated the marquis heartily.

The cat, going in advance all the way, said the same thing to

everyone he met, and the king was astonished at the great wealth of the Marquis of Carabas.

At last the cat came to a fine castle whose master was an Ogre, the richest that was ever seen, for all the lands through which the king had passed were part of the castle grounds. The cat, who had taken pains to find out all about the Ogre and what he could do, asked to speak to him, saying that he was unwilling to pass so near his castle without having the honour to pay his respects. The Ogre received him as civilly as an Ogre can, and offered him a seat.

'I am told,' said the cat, 'that you have the power to change yourself into all sorts of animals: that you can, for example, turn yourself into a lion or an elephant.'

'That's true,' said the Ogre shortly; 'and to prove it, you shall see me become a lion.'

The cat was so frightened at seeing a lion before him that he instantly sprang up to the roof, not without difficulty and danger because of his boots, which were no good for walking on the tiles.

Some time after, the cat, seeing that the Ogre had resumed his former shape, came down again and confessed that he had been in a terrible fright.

'I have been told also,' he said, 'but I can hardly believe it, that you have the power of taking the form of the very smallest animals: for instance, a rat or a mouse. I confess that I regard that as altogether impossible.'

'Impossible?' roared the Ogre. 'You shall see.'

And in a moment he changed himself into a mouse and began to run over the floor. The cat had no sooner perceived him than he leapt upon him and crunched him up.

Meanwhile the king, seeing the Ogre's fine castle as he passed, determined to go inside. Puss, who heard the rumble of the wheels as the coach crossed the drawbridge, ran to meet it, and said to the king: 'Welcome, Your Majesty, to the castle of the Marquis of Carabas.'

'What, Marquis,' cried the king, 'this castle is yours? I have seen nothing finer than this courtyard and all the buildings round it: let us see the interior, if you please.'

The marquis gave his hand to the young princess, and walking

upstairs behind the king, they came to a splendid hall, where they found a magnificent feast which the Ogre had got ready for his friends. The king was charmed with the good qualities of the Marquis of Carabas; and his daughter, as I told you, was in love with him. Seeing his great wealth, the king, after drinking five or six glasses of wine, said to him: 'You have only to say the word, Marquis, and you shall be my son-in-law.'

The marquis, with very low bows, accepted the honour that the king did him; and that very day he married the princess.

Master Puss became a great lord, and henceforth only ran after mice for amusement.

9

Tom Thumb

Tom Thumb

Long ago, in the merry days of good King Arthur, there lived a ploughman and his wife. They were very poor, but would have been contented and happy if only they could have had a little child. One day, having heard of the great fame of the magician Merlin, who was living at the Court of King Arthur, the wife persuaded her husband to go and tell him of their trouble. Having arrived at the Court, the man besought Merlin with tears in his eyes to give them a child, saying that they would be quite content even though it should be no bigger than his thumb. Merlin determined to grant the request, and what was the countryman's astonishment to find when he reached home that his wife had a son, who, wonderful to relate, was no bigger than his father's thumb!

The parents were now very happy, and the christening of the little fellow took place with great ceremony. The Fairy Queen, attended by all her company of elves, was present at the feast. She kissed the little child, and, giving it the name of Tom Thumb, told her fairies to fetch the tailors of her Court, who dressed her little godson according to her orders. His hat was made of a beautiful oak leaf, his shirt of a fine spider's web, and his hose and doublet were of thistledown, his stockings were made with the rind of a delicate green apple, and the garters were two of the finest little hairs imaginable, plucked from his mother's eyebrows, while his shoes were made of the skin of a little mouse. When he

was thus dressed, the Fairy Queen kissed him once more, and, wishing him all good luck, flew off with the fairies to her Court.

As Tom grew older, he became very amusing and full of tricks, so that his mother was afraid to let him out of her sight. One day, while she was making a batter pudding, Tom stood on the edge of the bowl, with a lighted candle in his hand, so that she might see that the pudding was made properly. Unfortunately, however, when her back was turned, Tom fell into the bowl, and his mother, not missing him, stirred him up in the pudding, tied it in a cloth, and put it into the pot. The batter filled Tom's mouth, and prevented him from calling out, but he had no sooner felt the hot water, than he kicked and struggled so much that the pudding jumped about in the pot, and his mother, thinking the pudding was bewitched, was nearly frightened out of her wits. Pulling it out of the pot, she ran with it to the door, and gave it to a tinker who was passing. He was very thankful for it, and looked forward to having a better dinner than he had enjoyed for many a long day.

But his pleasure did not last long, for, as he was getting over a stile, he happened to sneeze very hard, and Tom, who had been quite quiet inside the pudding for some time, called out at the top of his little voice, 'Hallo, Pickens!' This so terrified the tinker that he flung away the pudding, and ran off as fast as he could. The pudding was all broken to pieces by the fall, and Tom crept out, covered with batter, and ran home to his mother, who had been looking everywhere for him, and was delighted to see him again. She gave him a bath in a cup, which soon washed off all the pudding, and he was none the worse for his adventure.

A few days after this, Tom accompanied his mother when she went into the fields to milk the cows, and, fearing he might be

blown away by the wind, she tied him to a sow-thistle with a little piece of thread. While she was milking, a cow came by, bit off the thistle, and swallowed up Tom. Poor Tom did not like her big teeth, and called out loudly, 'Mother, mother!'

'But where are you, Tommy, my dear Tommy?' cried out his mother, wringing her hands.

'Here, mother,' he shouted, 'inside the red cow's mouth!' And, saying that, he began to kick and scratch till the poor cow was nearly mad, and at length tumbled him out of her mouth. On seeing this, his mother rushed to him, caught him in her arms, and carried him safely home.

Some days after this, his father took him to the fields a-ploughing, and gave him a whip, made of barley straw, with which to drive the oxen; but little Tom was soon lost in a furrow. An eagle, seeing him, picked him up and flew with him to the top of a hill where stood a giant's castle. The giant put him at once into his mouth, intending to swallow him up, but Tom made such a great disturbance when he got inside that the monster was soon glad to get rid of him, and threw him far away into the sea. But he was not drowned, for he had scarcely touched the water before he was swallowed by a large fish, which was shortly afterwards

captured and brought to King Arthur, as a present, by the fisher-
man. When the fish was opened, everyone was astonished at
finding Tom inside. He was at once carried to the king, who made
him his Court dwarf.

> *Long time he lived in jollity,*
> *Belovèd of all the Court,*
> *And none like Tom was so esteemed*
> *Amongst the better sort.*

The queen was delighted with the little boy, and made him dance a galliard on her left hand. He danced so well that King Arthur gave him a ring, which he wore round his waist like a girdle.

Tom soon began to long to see his parents again, and begged the king to allow him to go home for a short time. This was readily permitted, and the king told him he might take with him as much money as he could carry.

> *And so away goes lusty Tom,*
> *With three pence at his back—*
> *A heavy burthen which did make*
> *His very bones to crack.*

He had to rest more than a hundred times by the way, but, after two days and two nights, he reached his father's house in safety. His mother saw him coming, and ran out to meet him, and there was great rejoicing at his arrival. He spent three happy days at home, and then set out for the Court once more.

Shortly after his return, he one day displeased the king, so, fearing the royal anger, he crept into an empty flower-pot, where he lay for a long time. At last he ventured to peep out, and, seeing a fine large butterfly on the ground close by, he stole out of his hiding-place, jumped on its back, and was carried up into the air. The king and nobles all strove to catch him, but at last poor Tom fell from his seat into a watering-pot, in which he was almost drowned, only luckily the gardener's child saw him, and pulled him out. The king was so pleased to have him safe once more that he forgot to scold him, and made much of him instead.

Tom afterwards lived many years at Court, one of the best beloved of King Arthur's knights.

> *Thus he at tilt and tournament*
> *Was entertainèd so,*
> *That all the rest of Arthur's knights*
> *Did him much pleasure show.*
> *With good Sir Launcelot du Lake,*
> *Sir Tristram and Sir Guy,*
> *Yet none compared to brave Tom Thumb*
> *In acts of chivalry.*

10

*The Story of the Three
Little Pigs*

The Story of the Three Little Pigs

Once upon a time there was an old sow with three little pigs, and as she had not enough to keep them she sent them out to seek their fortune. The first that went off met a man with a bundle of straw, and said to him:

'Please, man, give me that straw to build me a house.'

Which the man did, and the little pig built a house with it. Presently along came a wolf, and knocked at the door, and said: 'Little pig, little pig, let me come in.'

To which the pig answered:

'No, no, by the hair of my chinny chin chin.'

The wolf then answered to that:

'Then I'll huff, and I'll puff, and I'll blow your house in.'

So he huffed, and he puffed, and he blew his house in, and ate up the little pig.

The second little pig met a man with a bundle of furze, and said:

'Please, man, give me that furze to build a house.'

Which the man did, and the pig built his house. Then along came the wolf, and said:

'Little pig, little pig, let me come in.'

'No, no, by the hair of my chinny chin chin.'

'Then I'll puff, and I'll huff, and I'll blow your house in.'

So he huffed, and he puffed, and he puffed, and he huffed, and at last he blew the house down, and he ate up the little pig.

The third little pig met a man with a load of bricks, and said: 'Please, man, give me those bricks to build a house with.'

So the man gave him the bricks, and he built his house with them. So the wolf came, as he did to the other little pigs, and said:

'Little pig, little pig, let me come in.'

'No, no, by the hair of my chinny chin chin.'

'Then I'll huff, and I'll puff, and I'll blow your house in.'

Well, he huffed, and he puffed, and he huffed, and he puffed, and he puffed, and he huffed; but he could *not* get the house down. When he found that he could not, with all his huffing and puffing, blow the house down, he said:

'Little pig, I know where there is a nice field of turnips.'

'Where?' said the little pig.

'Oh, in Mr Smith's Home-field, and if you will be ready tomorrow morning I will call for you, and we will go together and get some for dinner.'

'Very well,' said the little pig, 'I will be ready. What time do you mean to go?'

'Oh, at six o'clock.'

Well, the little pig got up at five, and got the turnips himself. Then, about six, along came the wolf, and he said:

'Little pig, are you ready?'

The little pig said: 'Ready! I have been and come back again, and got a nice potful for dinner.'

The wolf felt very angry at this, but thought that he would be up to the little pig somehow or other, so he said:

'Little pig, I know where there is a nice apple tree.'

'Where?' said the pig.

'Down at Merry Garden,' replied the wolf, 'and if you will not deceive me, I will come for you at five o'clock tomorrow, and we will go together and get some apples.'

Well, the little pig bustled up the next morning at four o'clock, and went off for the apples, hoping to get back before the wolf came: but he had farther to go, and had to climb the tree, so that, just as he was coming down from it, he saw the wolf coming, which, as you may suppose, frightened him very much. When the wolf came up he said:

'Little pig, what, are you here before me? Are they nice apples?'

'Yes, very,' said the little pig. 'I will throw you down one.'

And he threw it so far, that, while the wolf was gone to pick it up, the little pig jumped down and ran home. The next day the wolf came again, and said to the little pig:

'Little pig, there is a fair at Shanklin this afternoon; will you go?'

'Oh yes,' said the pig, 'I will go; what time shall you be ready?'

'At three,' said the wolf. So the little pig went off before the time as usual, and got to the fair, and bought a butter-churn,

which he was going home with, when he saw the wolf coming.
Then he could not tell what to do. So he got into the churn to
hide, and by so doing turned it round, and it rolled down the hill
with the pig in it, which frightened the wolf so much that he ran
home without going to the fair. He went to the little pig's house
and told him how frightened he had been by a great round thing
which came down the hill past him. Then the little pig said:

'Ha! I frightened you, then, did I? I had been to the fair and
bought a butter-churn, and when I saw you, I got into it, and
rolled down the hill.'

Then the wolf was very angry indeed, and declared he *would* eat up the little pig, and that he would get down the chimney after him. When the little pig saw what he was about, he put on the pot, full of water, and made up a blazing fire, and, just as the wolf was coming down, took off the cover, and in fell the wolf; so the little pig put on the cover again in an instant, boiled him up, and ate him for supper, and lived happily ever afterwards.